MW01026103

Dear Parent:
Your child's love of reading starts here!

Every child learns to read in a different way and at his or her own speed. You can help your young reader improve and become more confident by encouraging his or her own interests and abilities. You can also guide your child's spiritual development by reading stories with biblical values and Bible stories, like I Can Read! books published by Zonderkidz. From books your child reads with you to the first books he or she reads alone, there are I Can Read! books for every stage of reading:

SHARED READING
Basic language, word repetition, and whimsical illustrations, ideal for sharing with your emergent reader.

BEGINNING READING
Short sentences, familiar words, and simple concepts for children eager to read on their own.

READING WITH HELP
Engaging stories, longer sentences, and language play for developing readers.

READING ALONE
Complex plots, challenging vocabulary, and high-interest topics for the independent reader.

ADVANCED READING
Short paragraphs, chapters, and exciting themes for the perfect bridge to chapter books.

I Can Read! books have introduced children to the joy of reading since 1957. Featuring award-winning authors and illustrators and a fabulous cast of beloved characters, I Can Read! books set the standard for beginning readers.

A lifetime of discovery begins with the magical words **"I Can Read!"**

Visit www.icanread.com for information on enriching your child's reading experience.
Visit www.zonderkidz.com for more Zonderkidz I Can Read! titles.

MADE BY GOD

WEIRD & WONDERFUL CREATIONS

ZONDERKIDZ

Weird and Wonderful Creations

This title is also available as a Zondervan ebook.
Visit www.zondervan.com/ebooks.

Requests for information should be addressed to:

Zonderkidz, *3900 Sparks Drive SE, Grand Rapids, Michigan 49546*

Library of Congress Cataloging-in-Publication Data

Weird and wonderful creations.
pages cm. — (Made by God)
Compilation of four previously published works.
Includes index.
ISBN 978-0-310-73124-5 (hardcover) — ISBN 978-0-310-73121-4 (epub)—
ISBN 978-0-310-73082-8 (epub) — ISBN 978-0-310-73091-0 (epub)
1. Animals—Miscellanea —Juvenile literature. 2. Plants—Miscellanea —
Juvenile literature.
QH48.W38 2014
590—dc23 2014014303

Editor: Mary Hassinger
Cover and interior design: Cindy Davis

Printed in Hong Kong

14 15 16 17 18 /PEH/ 10 9 8 7 6 5 4 3 2 1

TABLE OF CONTENTS

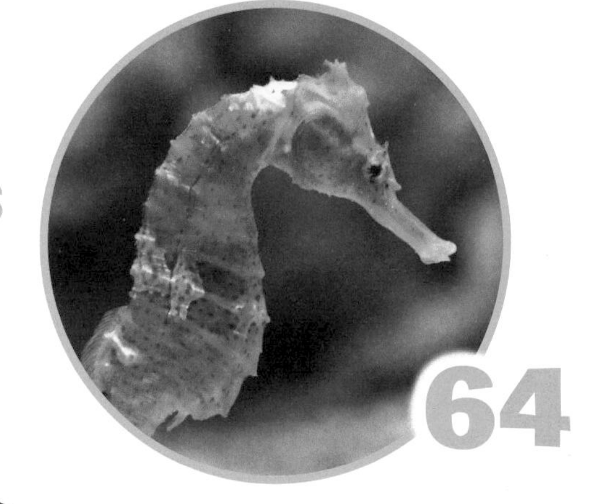

SPIDERS, SNAKES, BEES, AND BATS

Many people are scared of spiders, snakes, bees, and bats.

Spiders, snakes, bees, and bats are all helpful creatures. They do things like: eat pests and pollinate plants to help them grow. God had a great plan when he made them.

There are spiders, snakes, and bats that people have not discovered yet.

SPIDER!

Spiders are found on every continent except Antarctica.

Spiders do not have antennae.

The fear of spiders is called *arachnophobia.*

Only a few spiders in North America are really dangerous to humans.

Spiders are not really insects.

They are animals called arachnids.

Spiders are found almost everywhere.

Spiders have
fangs that shoot
venom into their food.

God made about 30,000 kinds
of spiders.
Most have eight legs and eight eyes.
Spiders are carnivorous.
They eat only meat.

Spiders might be pests,
but they eat many bugs that bug us,
like mosquitoes.
To help catch food, most spiders
use webs.

Young spiders ride the wind on long silk threads. This is called *ballooning*.

Trapdoor spiders dig tunnels in the ground and close the opening with a trapdoor.

Spider body parts called spinnerets make silk to build webs. Webs are used as homes, to catch food, and for cocoons. There are many kinds of webs—spiral orb and funnel are two.

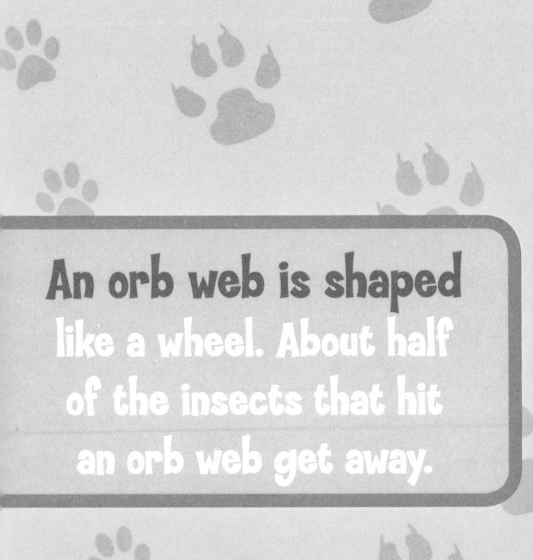

Most spiders live only for a year or two, but tarantulas can live up to 25 years in captivity!

A well-known spider is
the tarantula.
Tarantulas are furry.
They can grow to be nine or ten
inches—like a dinner plate!
Some people have pet tarantulas.

The largest spider in the world is called the giant huntsman spider. It can grow to be 12 inches!

God made everything.

It is all good.

He made the cutest puppy

and the longest, creepiest …

SNAKE!

Snakes are cold-blooded. This means they need the sun in order to stay warm.

Some snakes have *infrared receptors*. That means they can sense the heat of nearby animals.

Snakes do not
live in Ireland.

Snakes are reptiles.
They are found almost
everywhere.
Snakes live in deserts, lakes,
forests, and fields.

Snakes are covered with smooth,
dry scales that protect them.
Snakes shed their old scales.
If they do not fall off,
the snake might get sick.

Some snakes live in the water and have a flat tail that helps them swim.

Before a snake sheds its skin, its eyes become cloudy or blue-colored.

Rattlesnakes use a rattle at the end of their tail to warn predators. The noise comes from hollow bony pieces in the rattle banging together.

Some snakes are hatched from eggs.
Others come out of their mother.
No matter how they are born,
all snakes have special bones that
twist, bend, and curl.

A King cobra has special muscles and ribs in its neck. When it feels threatened, it spreads these muscles out to look bigger.

Snakes smell with their tongues.
The tongue collects smells.
It goes back into the snake's mouth
to a spot called Jacobson's Organ.
It tells the snake whose scent
is on the tongue.

Snakes do not usually attack humans unless they are scared or injured.

Many snakes can eat prey three times larger than their head. Their lower jaw can separate from their upper jaw.

The reticulated python is the world's longest snake. It can grow up to 30 feet!

One very tiny snake is called
a thread snake.
It eats ant and termite eggs.
The longest snakes are
pythons and anacondas.
They eat eggs, fish, frogs, and
small rodents.
If they eat a big meal, these snakes
eat only four or five times a year!

God made everything.

It is all good.

He made the prettiest rose

and the buzzing, stinging …

Snakes hunt mostly at night.

Boa constrictors kill their prey by wrapping around it and squeezing tightly.

People called *beekeepers* raise bees in order to collect their honey.

Many species of honeybees are disappearing. Scientists are not sure why.

BEE!

Bees are insects.

They have six legs, five eyes, four wings, a nectar pouch, and stomach.

Bees are found in many places but do not like cold weather.

In winter, bees stay in their hive to keep warm.

They eat the honey they made all summer.

Bees see all colors except red.

Some species of bees die after they sting.

If a queen dies, workers feed one of the female workers a special food called "royal jelly." This turns her into a new queen that can lay eggs.

Bees have a long "tongue" that helps them drink nectar from flowers.

God made more than 10,000 kinds of bees.

Bees live in hives or nests.

A small hive may have 20,000 bees!

There is only one queen, and she is in charge for two to three years.

The queen bee can lay

2,000 eggs every day.

She has lots of help in the hive.

Female worker bees do all the work.

There are hundreds of male bees

called drones.

The drones have no stingers.

Their main job is to help the queen

make babies.

All bees have two pairs of wings.

Only female bees sting.

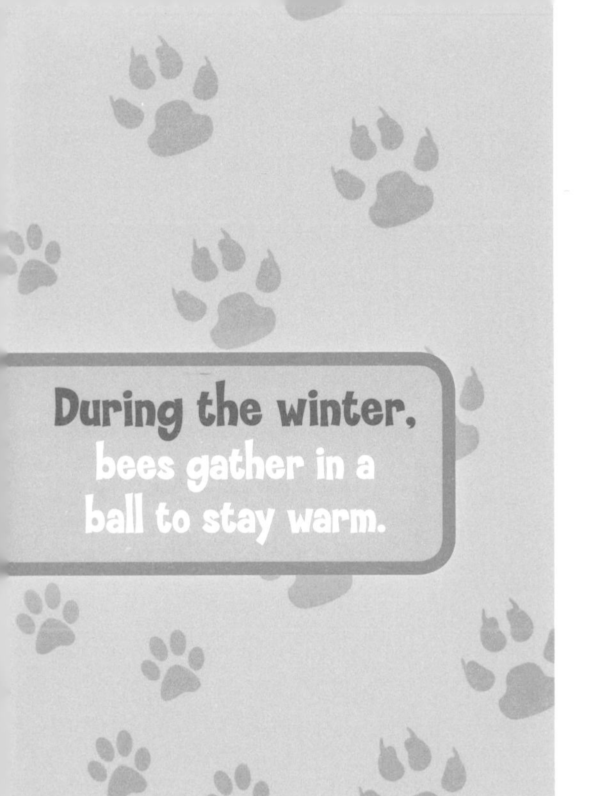

During the winter, bees gather in a ball to stay warm.

Most pollen is used as food for *larvae*. Larvae are baby bees.

Bees have two jobs.
Bees make honey from
pollen and nectar in flowers.
One bee visits 4,000 flowers
to make one tablespoon of honey!
When looking for pollen,
a bee can fly six miles and
travel fifteen miles an hour!

Bees' most common predators are birds and dragonflies.

Most bees are fuzzy. This helps pollen stick to them.

Bees have a job called pollination.
Their sticky legs help pollen
get from one plant to another.
Without the help of bees,
many plants may not grow.

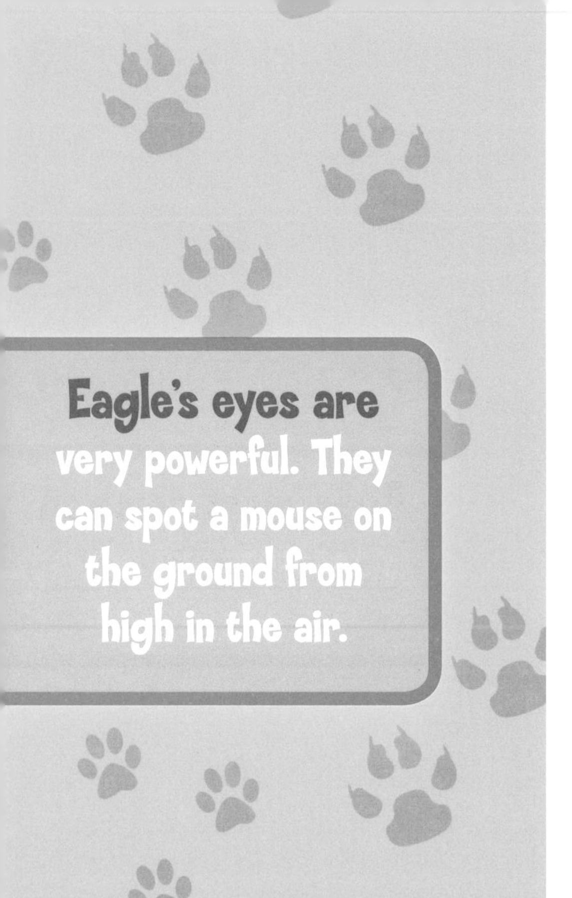

Eagle's eyes are very powerful. They can spot a mouse on the ground from high in the air.

The bones in a bat's wings are similar to the bones in a human's hand.

God made everything.

It is all good.

He made the big, strong eagle

and the squeaky, scary-looking …

BAT!

Bats can hear and smell very well. But they have poor eyesight.

Bats eat pests like the corn earworm moth. This moth attacks crops like watermelon.

The tube-lipped nectar bat has the longest tongue of any mammal for its body size. It uses its long tongue to reach deep into flowers.

Many bats can live up to twenty years.

Bats are the only flying mammal in the world.
They use their wings for flying and holding things like food.

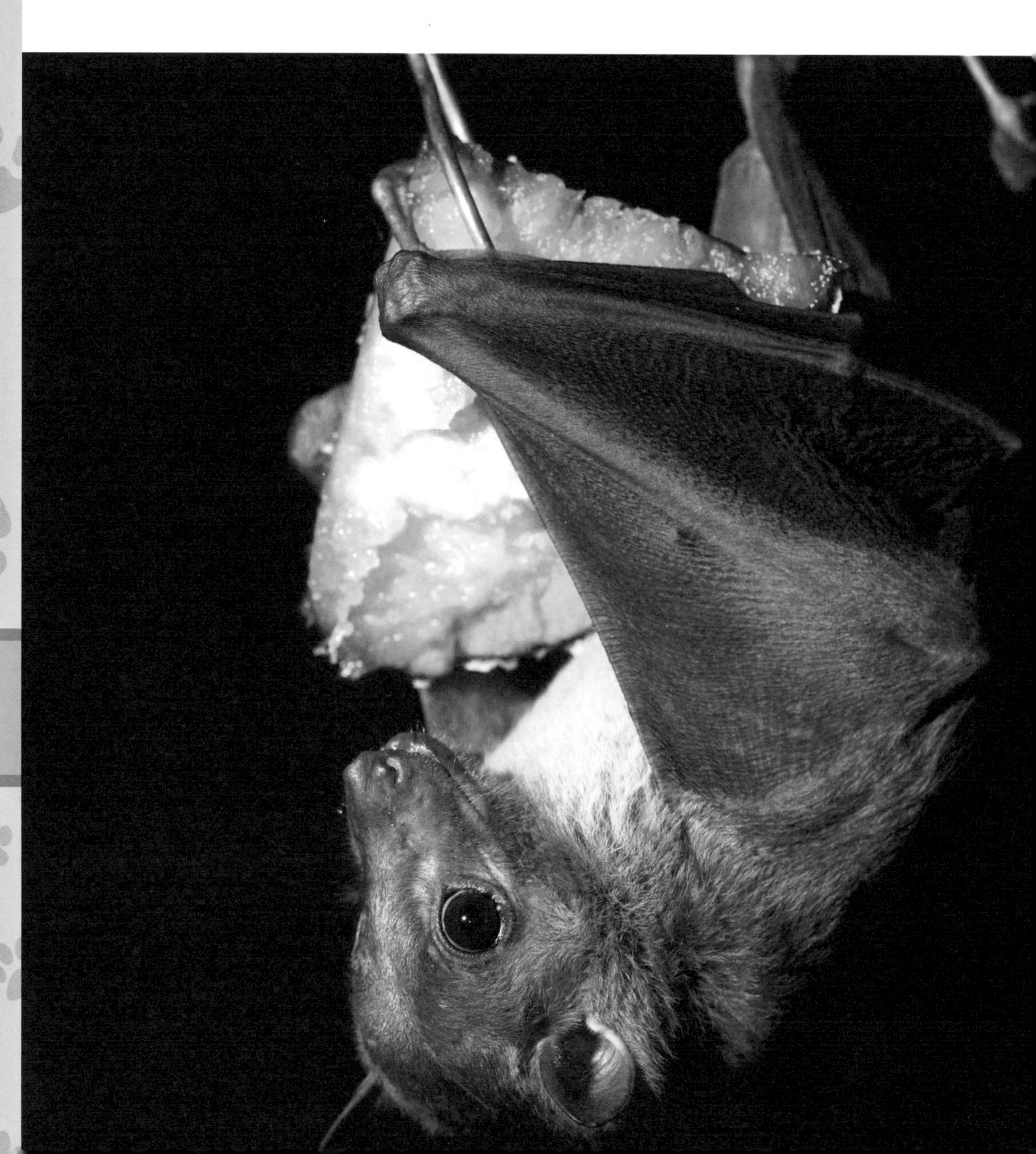

A bat's home is called a *roost.*

God made over 1,000 kinds of bats.
They live all over the world.
Bats sleep in roosts.
Roosts are found in places
like caves and hollow trees.
Bats sleep upside-down.
This makes it easier for them to
take off fast, if necessary.

To survive the cold winter, some species of bats migrate to warmer places. Others hibernate.

Bats help people by eating
pesky bugs like mosquitoes.
A single brown bat can eat 1,200
mosquitoes in one hour!
Other bats eat fruit, fish, and frogs.
Bats mostly eat at night.
They use sounds that people cannot
hear to help find food in the dark.
This is called echo-location.

A few species of bats eat mainly blood. These are called vampire bats.

Usually, a bat will use its wings or tail to trap an insect in a kind of "bug net." Then the bat will take the insect back to its roost to eat it.

Bat babies are called pups.

When bats grow up, they like to live and fly in large groups called colonies.

One of the largest colonies of bats
is in the state of Texas.
About twenty million bats
live together in one cave and share
a dinner of about 200 tons of bugs …
each night!

BIG BUGS, LITTLE BUGS

There are between six and ten million kinds of insects in the world!

Insects are found nearly everywhere—even in the ocean!

God made it all,

and he made it all good.

He made bees that sting,

ants that crawl,

and the gentle flying …

You can tell a bug is an insect if it has:

- a three-part body
- three pairs of legs
- one pair of antennae

BUTTERFLIES!

Butterflies begin life as caterpillars. After they grow big and fat, they hang from a leaf or branch and change into a hard chrysalis. Then they turn into a butterfly.

Butterflies drink nectar through their tongues which act like straws.

God put butterflies
all over the world.
But not where it is very cold.
Some butterflies fly up to
2,000 miles to find
a warm place to live.

During the night or bad weather, butterflies often hang upside down from leaves and sleep.

Butterflies can smell using their feet, legs, and antennae.

There are about

18,000 kinds of butterflies!

The Pygmy Blue is the smallest butterfly. Its wingspan is only half an inch.

Queen Alexandra's Birdwing is the largest and rarest butterfly.

Some kinds are:

Monarch

Tiger swallowtail

Zebra swallowtail

Goliath birdwing

Butterfly wings are
covered with tiny scales.

Butterflies live in groups
called flutters.
They live six to eight months
and grow from 1/8-inch wide to
12 inches wide.
Butterflies can fly up to 12
miles an hour!

Some butterflies
have eyespots on their wings. This confuses their enemies.

God blessed butterflies with
colorful wings.
These colors help protect
and hide them from danger.

Butterflies have four wings.

Some male butterflies like to drink from mud puddles.

God made butterflies very colorful,

but he made another bug

that is almost always

black and white …

GOLIATH BEETLE

The Goliath beetle was named after the giant in the Bible named Goliath.

Some people keep Goliath beetles as pets!

Female Goliath beetles do not have a horn. Instead, they have a wedge-shaped head that helps them dig holes in which to lay eggs.

Beetles have a hard covering over their wings called an *elytra*. This helps protect them.

The Goliath beetle is the largest beetle in the world. They are two to four inches long and weigh three to four ounces.

The goliath beetle can be
found in tropical parts of Africa.
They use their sharp, strong claws
to climb trees and branches
to find sap and fruit to eat.

The Goliath beetle's leathery wings can be larger than a sparrow's.

The male beetle has a Y-shaped
horn that it uses to
help fight for food it finds
in the trees.

The goliath beetle can fly.
Their strong wings make them
sound like a helicopter!

These beetles also eat dead animals and animal dung.

Goliath beetle larvae eat other insects, which is odd.

God made the very large
goliath beetle.
He made a much smaller beetle too.
He made the bright, little …

LIGHTNING BUG!

Many lightning bugs live in marshes or wet, wooded areas.

Lightning bugs are nocturnal, which means they are most active at night.

Female fireflies lay their eggs on or just below the surface of the ground.

Lightning bugs are a type of beetle.

Lightning bugs are also called fireflies.
There are 2,000 kinds of lightning bugs.
They live from two months to a year.

Lightning bugs can grow to be about one inch long—as big as a paperclip.

Lightning bugs do not taste good to most of their predators.

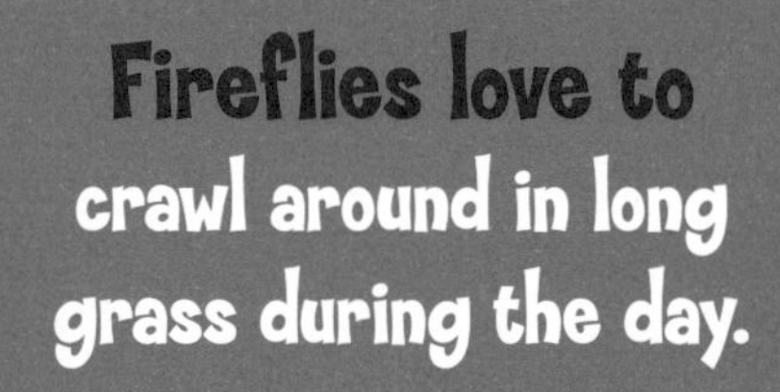

Each species of firefly has its own special light flashing pattern.

Lightning bug larvae that emit light are often called "glowworms."

Fireflies have special body parts that make them glow. When they glow, the bugs are talking to each other, attracting other bugs, or trying to scare other bugs away.

Adult fireflies are not
the only ones that glow.
In some kinds, the larvae and
eggs might even glow!
Long ago, in China,
people caught fireflies to
make lanterns.

Scientists think that light from humans, like car headlights, can interrupt firefly flashing patterns.

Fireflies hibernate over the winter when they are still "glowworms." They emerge in the spring and soon become adults.

When they are young, fireflies eat bugs like snails and other fireflies.

Scientists are not sure what adult fireflies eat—maybe nothing!

When God made lightning bugs,
he made them glow.
He made another bug that
would rather hide.
It is the …

Scientists call fireflies' light "cold light" because it does not make any heat.

Some species of fireflies live in the water.

PRAYING MANTIS!

A praying mantis can be tiny, but some are as big as a tea cup!

Praying mantises have wings, but they do not fly very often. They use their wings to scare enemies.

There are about 1,800 kinds of praying mantises. They live all over the world but not where it snows all the time.

The largest praying mantis ever was found in China. It was as long as your forearm!

A female lays hundreds of eggs at once. She coats the eggs with a hard foam to keep them wet and safe.

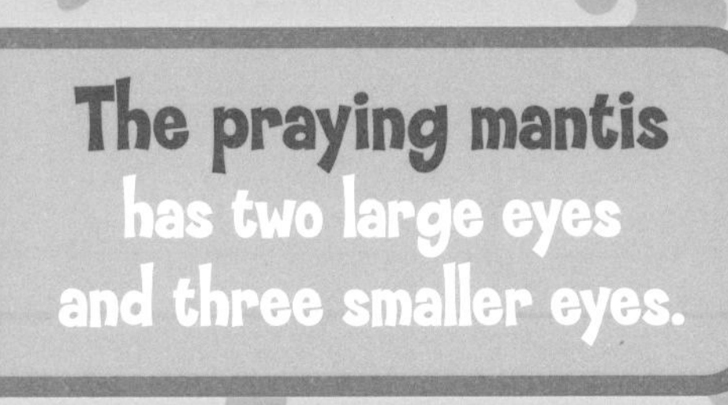

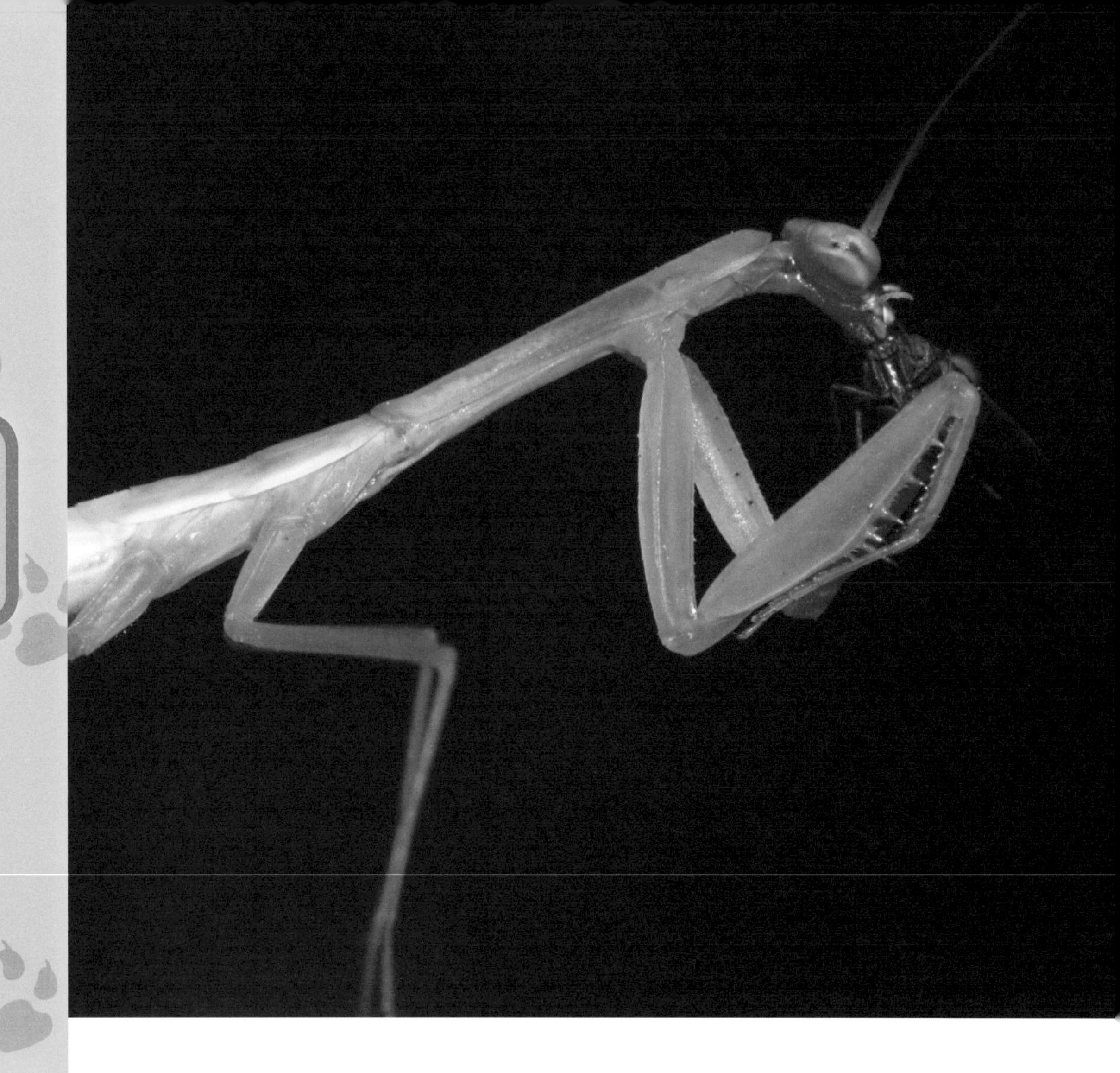

Some mantises are able to detect the *echolocation* sounds of bats. This helps them escape.

The praying mantis got its name because of how it looks. Its long front legs are bent up and together and look like someone praying!

The praying mantis is almost always green or brown.
This means it can hide on leaves or branches.
The head of the praying mantis can turn almost in a circle!

The praying mantis's most common enemies are bats, birds, frogs, and spiders.

A mantis has a very strong mouth for cutting through its food.

Mantises' legs have spikes that help them catch food.

Sometimes praying mantises will eat each other!

The color of the praying mantis
and the way it moves
make it easier for
this bug to catch its food of flies,
moths, crickets, and more.

God knew exactly what he was doing!

Praying mantises help keep gardens healthy and growing by catching many pests.

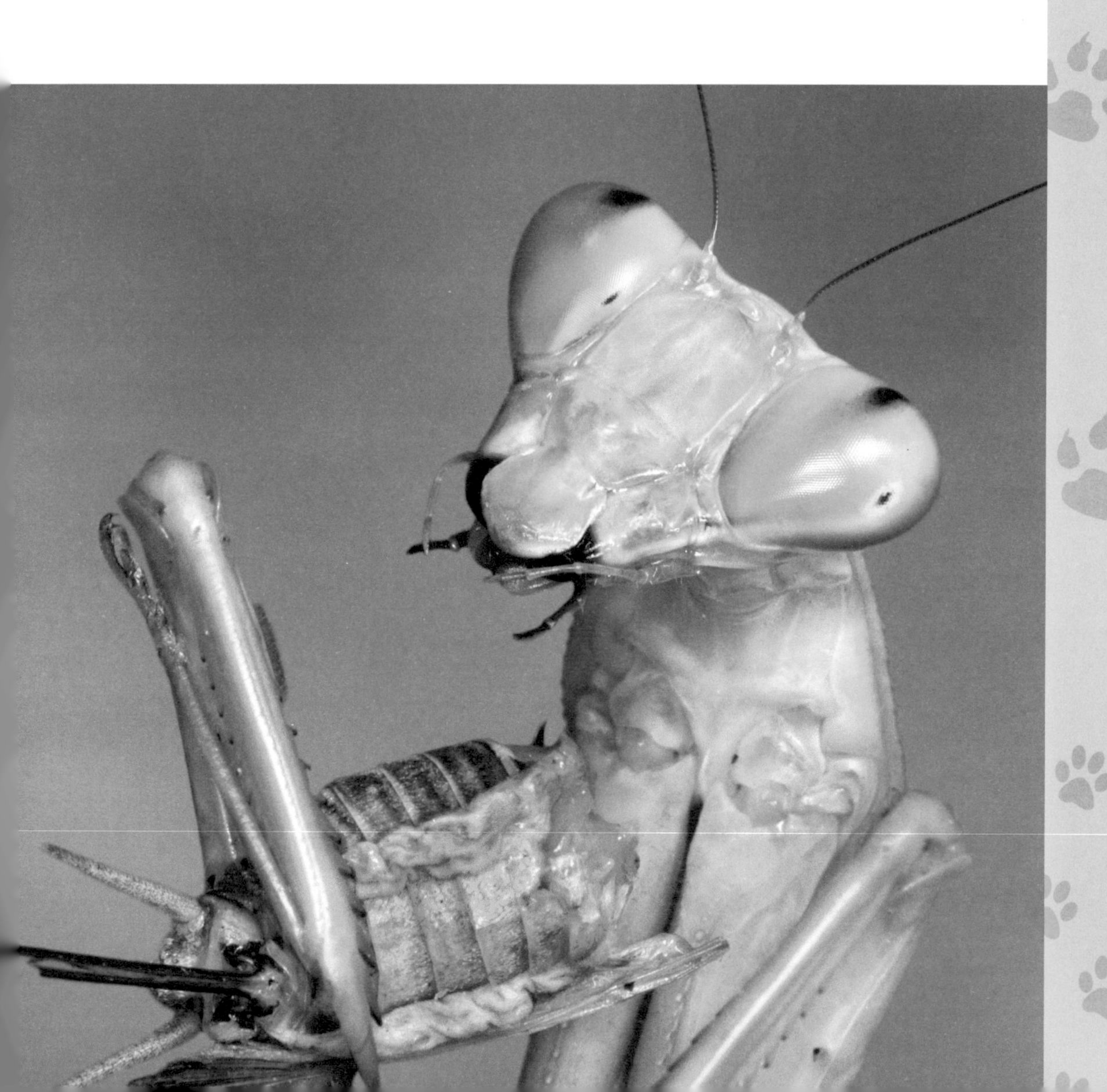

Baby mantises are called *nymphs*. They hatch looking just like tiny versions of their parents.

Some bugs are pests.

Some bugs are helpers.

But no matter what we think

of bugs, they are a special creation

from God!

The study of life in the ocean is called *marine biology*.

SEA CREATURES

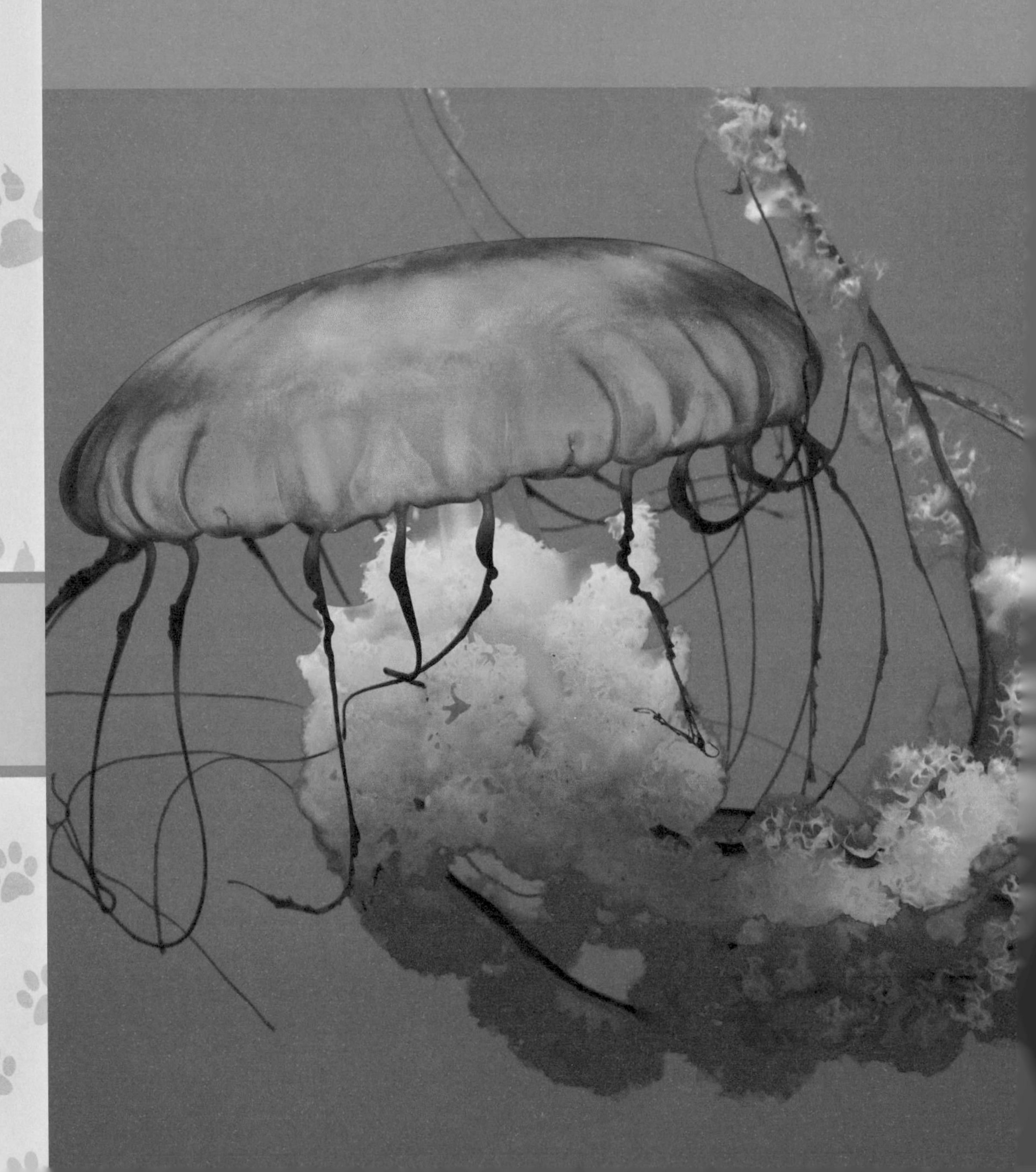

Oceans make up two-thirds of the earth's surface.

Between 700,000 and one million species live in the world's oceans.

God made everything,

and he made it all good.

He made the birds in the sky

and creatures under the sea,

like the …

Around half of the creatures in the sea haven't been identified yet.

JELLYFISH!

The rounded body of a jellyfish is sometimes called a bell.

Sea turtles love to eat jellyfish.

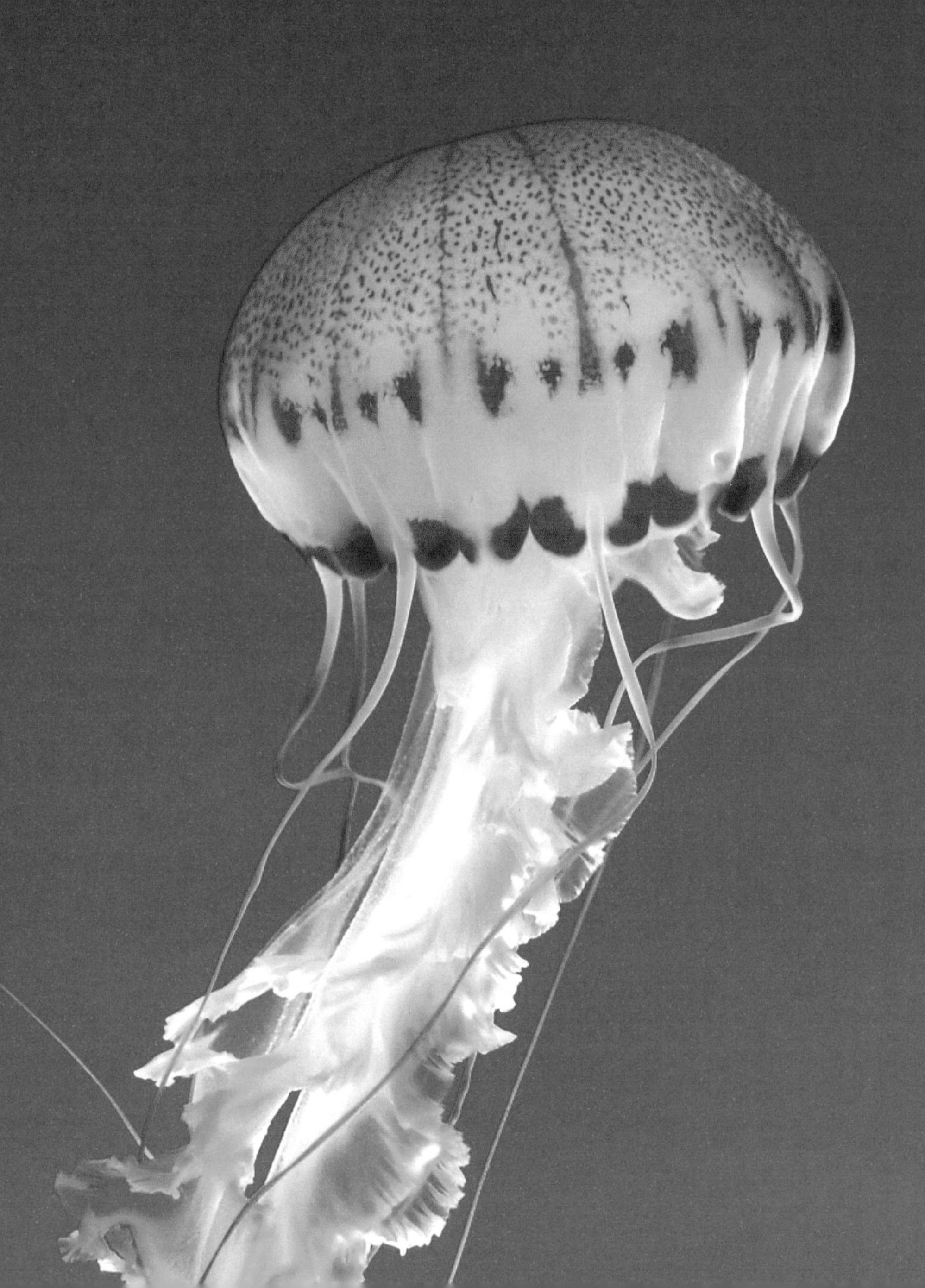

Jellyfish are not really fish.

They do not have bones.

They are more than 90% water.

Jellyfish look like see-through

umbrellas with long legs

called tentacles.

Most jellyfish
live in salt water.

Some jellyfish
are so see-through
they are almost invisible!

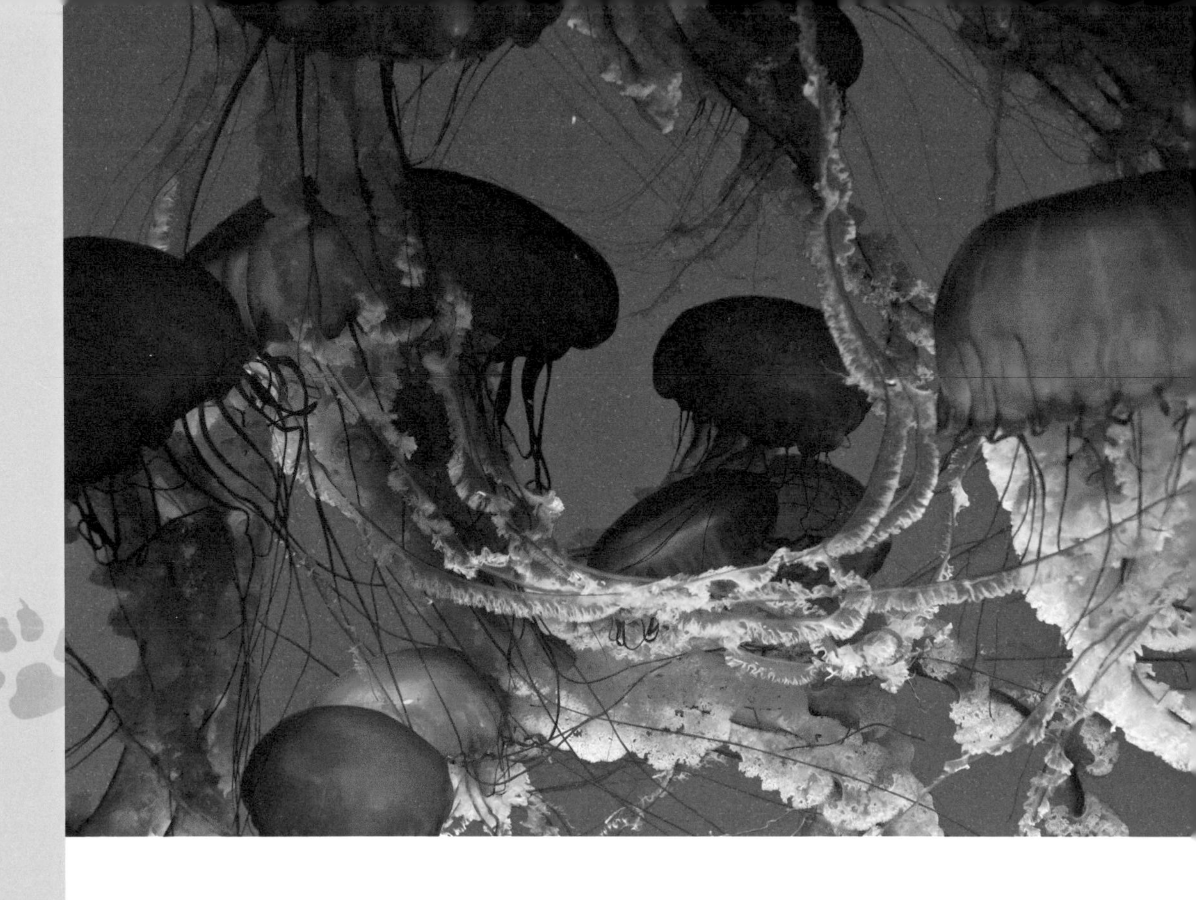

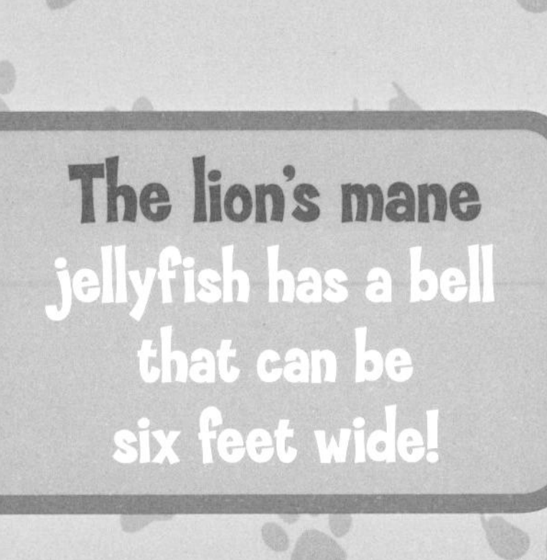

Jellyfish eat
shrimp, fish, tiny
plants, and even crabs.

There are more than
200 kinds of jellyfish.
Some are called:
Lion's mane jellyfish
Box jellyfish.
Jellyfish live in groups called
swarms or blooms.

Jellyfish float in the water.

Some move very quickly.

Jellyfish are in every ocean.

Some live near the top;

others live in the deep sea.

Jellyfish digest their food very quickly. If they didn't, they wouldn't be able to float very well!

Jellyfish move forward by squirting water from the same opening they use to eat.

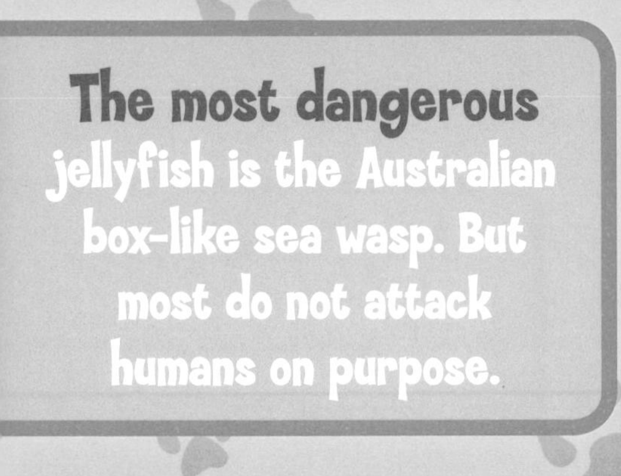

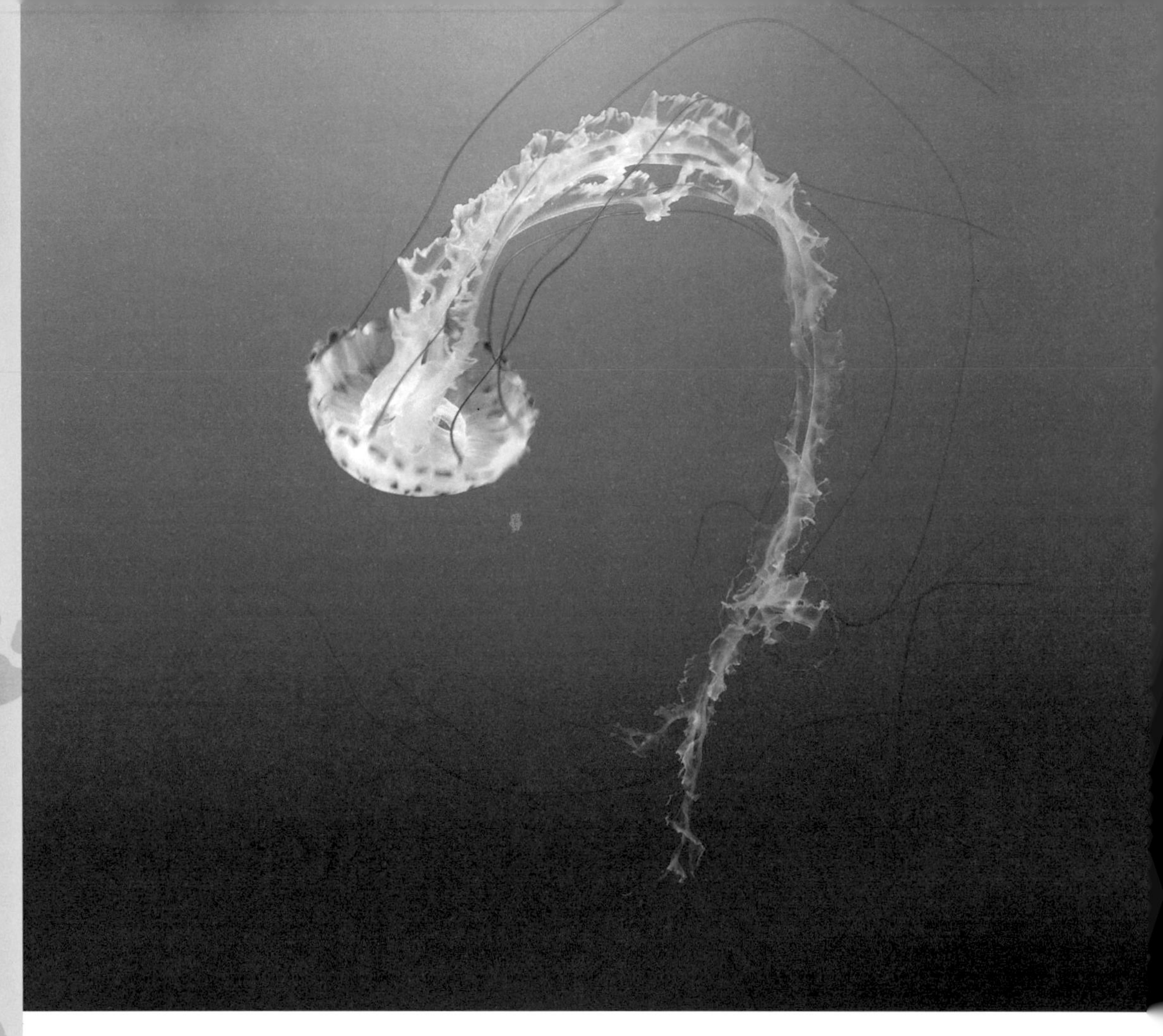

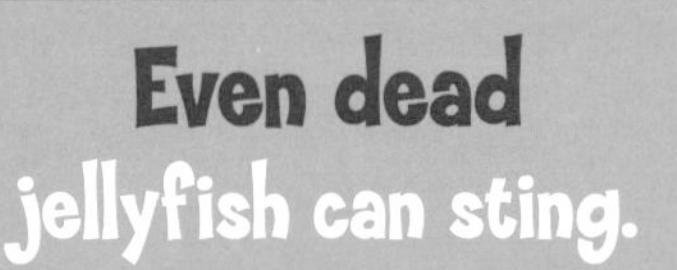

Jellyfish can be huge—120 feet long!

They can be poisonous.

Some of them sting!

Jellyfish only live

two to six months.

Even though jellyfish do not

have brains, hearts, or bones,

they are special to God,

just like …

Jellyfish come in all sorts of bright colors! Some even glow!

In some countries, jellyfish are a delicacy. That means people think they are tasty!

SEA HORSES!

Most sea horses can change color like a chameleon.

Sometimes sea horses travel long distances by hitching a ride on floating seaweed.

Sea horses are horse-shaped fish.
There are about 35 different kinds.
They live in shallow, warm,
tropical water.
Sea horses live one to five
years.
They only grow one-half
to fourteen inches long.

A sea horse uses its snout as a straw to suck up food.

Sometimes sea horses use their monkey-like tales to grab on to each other

The eyes of a sea horse can look in two directions at once.

Sea horses make clicking noises when they eat.

Sea horses have to eat almost all the time to stay alive. But they do not have teeth or stomachs!

Sea horses use their tails to
hold onto sea grass so they
can stay still to eat.
They eat plankton and fish eggs.

The smallest kind of sea horse is the pygmy seahorse. It is smaller than a dime!

Sea horses do not have scales. They have thin skin stretched over bony plates.

Sea horses are not good swimmers.
But they have a small fin
on their back
that flutters up to 35 times
in one second.
This helps them move better.

Another special sea horse fact
is that father sea horses
carry their babies
until they are born!

Sea horse couples greet each other every morning with a unique dance.

Since sea horses are mostly skin and bones, not many animals like to eat them.

Most sea horses have about 100 to 200 babies at a time!

God made many

special sea creatures!

He also made the amazing …

SEA TURTLE!

Sea turtles' flippers make them good swimmers.

Sea turtles get rid of extra salt in their bodies by crying.

Sometimes sea turtles get caught in fishing nets or fishing lines.

Even though sea turtles are protected, some people hunt them for their meat and skin.

There are seven kinds of sea turtles.

Some of them are:

Leatherback

Green turtle

Loggerhead

Kemp's ridley

Some sea turtles are in danger.
People do things that are not safe
for the turtles,
like pollute the water.
Even though sea turtles can
live for 80 years or more,
if people are not careful
sea turtles might all die.

Humans are the biggest threat to sea turtles, but some are also eaten by sharks.

Male sea turtles stay in the water their entire lives.

The green sea turtle can hold its breath for five hours!

Sea turtles often travel long distances from where they eat to where they lay their eggs.

Sea turtles live in all of the oceans, but not in frozen places. They are almost always under water but need to breathe air. When they are swimming, sea turtles eat jellyfish, seaweed, sponges, and algae.

Mother sea turtles come out
of the water to lay eggs in the sand.
They lay 50 to 100 eggs, bury them
in sand, and leave.
When the eggs hatch, the babies
run as fast as they can
to get to the water.

Mother sea turtles
return to the beach
where they were born
to lay their eggs.

The leatherback turtle can dive more than a thousand feet, looking for food. That's more than the length of three football fields!

Only about one in a thousand leatherback babies survive to adulthood.

The leatherback turtle is the
largest turtle in the world.
It can grow to be seven feet long,
three feet across, and 1,500 pounds.
Leatherbacks live in groups called bales.
They have soft shells.

God made sea turtles so
they cannot pull their heads into
their shells to hide
like other turtles!
God made another undersea creature
so big, they do not have to
hide either … it is the …

Many sea turtles have creatures called barnacles growing on their shell or skin.

Green sea turtles are like the lawn mowers of the ocean. They eat the sea grass and keep it short.

WHALE!

Whales are covered in a thick layer of fat to keep them warm in the cold ocean.

Some whales have teeth. Others have special structures in their mouths to strain food from the water.

Many kinds of
whales are endangered.

Whales are the largest animal
on earth.
They are mammals.
This means whales do things like
breathe air with their blowholes
and have live babies.

Baby blue whales
are already 25 feet long
when they are born!

There are over 80 kinds of whales.

Some are:

Hector dolphin—the smallest
at 39 inches

Blue whale—the largest
at 100 feet

Humpback whale

Beluga whale

Killer whale (orca)

Male whales are called bulls, and female whales are called cows. Baby whales are called calves.

Many whales eat only tiny creatures called krill.

Blue whales travel long distances, from the arctic all the way to Mexico!

Orcas work together to hunt food. They eat seals, fish, and penguins.

Whales live in every ocean.
They live in groups
called pods.
They are like a family.

Whales can talk to each other.
They use clicks and pings.
Whales can hear other whales
talk as far away as 100 miles!
Whales can swim fast to get
to each other—30 miles an hour.

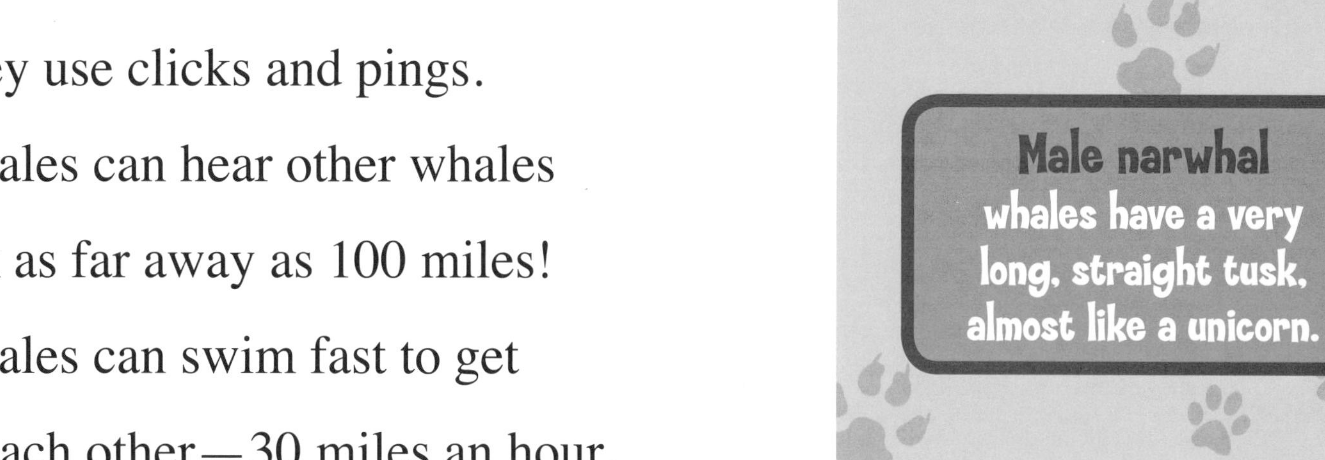

Male narwhal whales have a very long, straight tusk, almost like a unicorn.

Sperm whales have the largest brain of any animals on earth.

God made some underwater
creatures very huge.
He made some very small.
No matter the size or shape
of his creatures,
God made them all amazing!

The most common plant on earth is probably grass.

POISONOUS, SMELLY, AND AMAZING PLANTS

The South Pole, Greenland, and the North Pole have the fewest plants

In the rainforest, there are plants growing on plants growing on plants.

Some of the most special things
God made are called plants.
Some are poisonous,
some are smelly,
and some are just amazing.

Sometimes these mushrooms grow in circles. The circles are called fairy rings.

One special plant God made
is a mushroom called the fly agaric.
It is one of over fourteen thousand
kinds of mushrooms.

This mushroom likes to grow in the woods under trees.

Mushrooms come in all colors and shapes. The hedgehog mushroom looks like a furry animal!

The fly agaric grows mostly
in the northern half of the earth.
They can be found in other places too.
These mushrooms grow in groups.

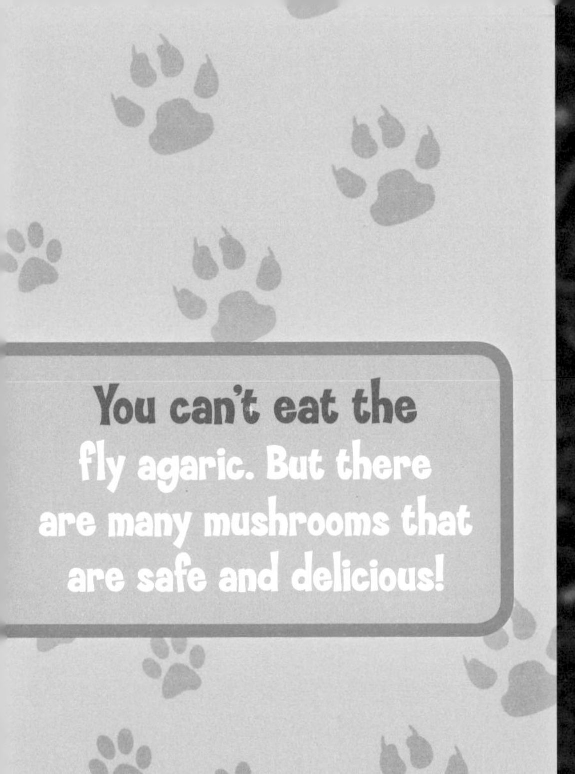

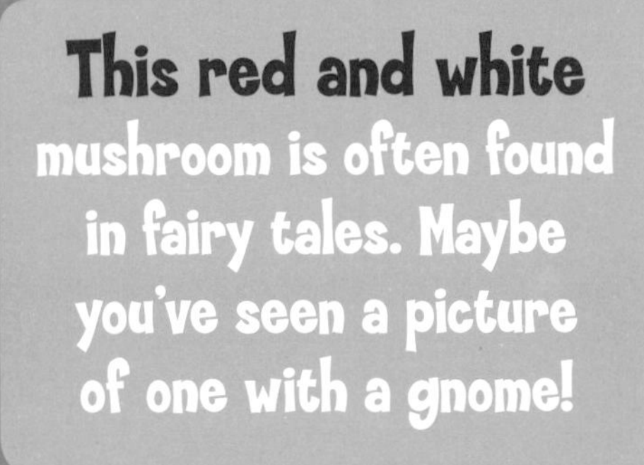

The fly agaric is poisonous.

It will make you sick if you eat it!

God made sure the fly agaric

would be noticed.

He made them look like bright

red umbrellas with white polka dots.

The tops of these mushrooms are about three to eight inches around. If you spot one, try to stay away.

Mushrooms grow quickly. Some seem to pop up overnight.

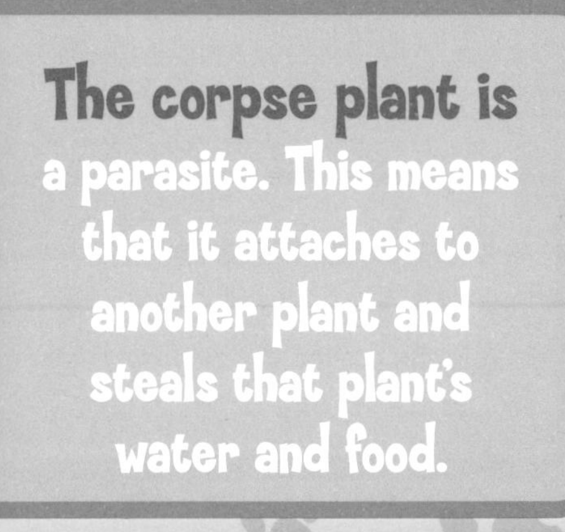

The center of this
flower contains
lots of spikes.

Another plant to stay away from
is very smelly.
It is called the corpse plant.
God made this plant smell
like rotten meat!
The flower is even red, like raw meat.

The terrible smell brings bugs
from miles away.
These bugs help the plant to grow
by pollinating it.

The corpse plant can hold several gallons of nectar.

These flowers are open for less than a week.

The corpse plant grows wild in the rainforests of Sumatra. Sumatra is an island north of Australia.

Greenhouses help plants grow by trapping the heat of the sun inside its walls.

It is also grown in special buildings called greenhouses.

The corpse plant also produces a round fruit.

God made the corpse plant one of
the biggest flower buds in the world—
some are four feet across!
This flower can grow
up to six inches in one day.

Some of these flowers are male and some are female.

This plant can hold several gallons of water.

The corpse plant
has no leaves, stem, or roots.
It is just a flower.

The Venus flytrap is another plant you might want to stay away from.

The Venus flytrap grows white flowers in the spring.

God made Venus flytraps
very special—they can bite!

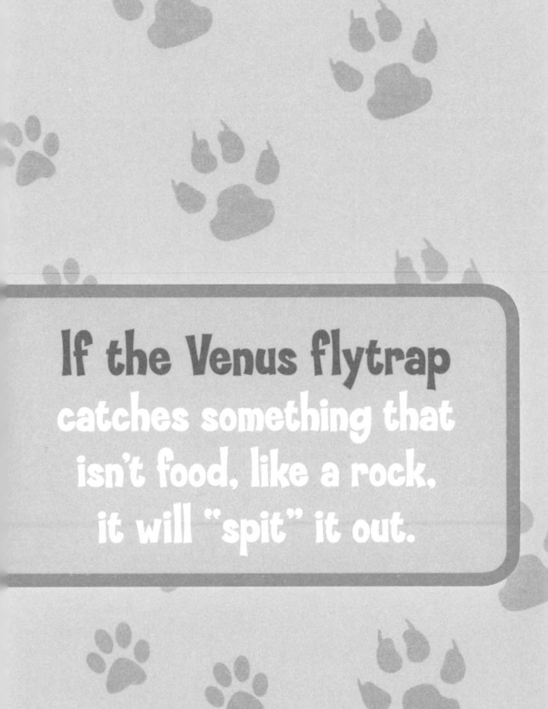

If the Venus flytrap catches something that isn't food, like a rock, it will "spit" it out.

The Venus flytrap does not want to catch bugs that are too small. It lets small bugs go.

Venus flytraps eat bugs.
The tiny trap of the plant
has small hairs.
When something touches the hair,
the trap will close
in less than one second!

It can take up to ten days
for a Venus flytrap to eat one bug.
They love flies, spiders, and crickets.

Venus flytraps can live for twenty or thirty years if they are cared for.

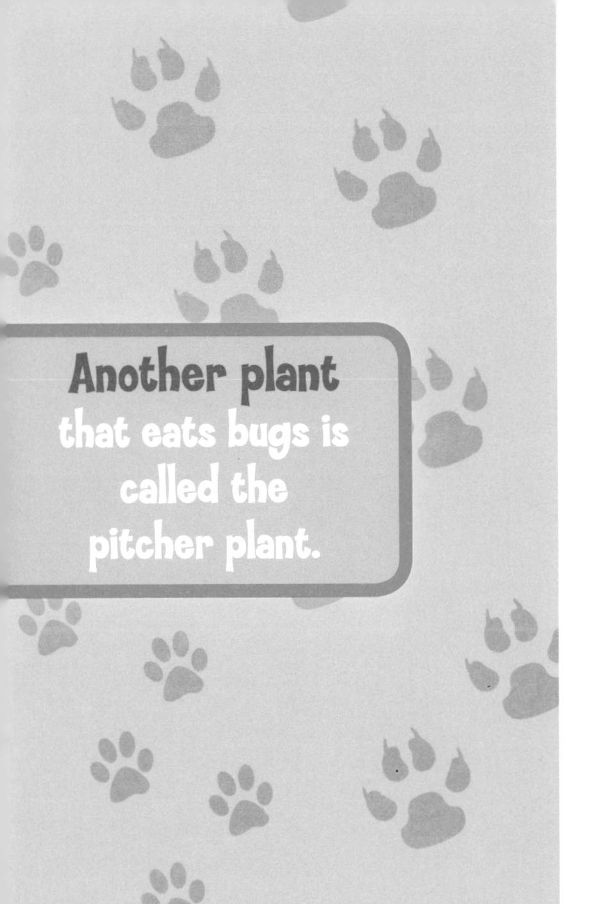

Venus flytraps grow wild in very few places—mostly in swamps and other humid places in North Carolina. You can buy a Venus flytrap at a flower nursery or store though.

The Venus flytrap never has more than seven leaves. If you see one with more than seven, that means it is really two plants!

This plant is known for being difficult to grow.

The Venus flytrap grows
to be four to six inches tall.
Its trap is about an inch long.
There is usually one trap
for each leaf on the plant.

God made the Venus flytrap
small but very special.
He also created huge plants.
One of them is an amazing tree
called a redwood.

Redwoods also love fog. Fog helps keep the soil wet.

Redwood trees are mostly found
in northern California.
These are huge trees!
A redwood might grow 400 feet high,
and up to 20 feet around.

When a redwood has plenty of food and water, it can grow two or three feet each year.

Redwood leaves are green, flat, and sharp.

The roots of
redwoods spread out and tangle with the roots of other redwoods. This helps them stay up when it is windy.

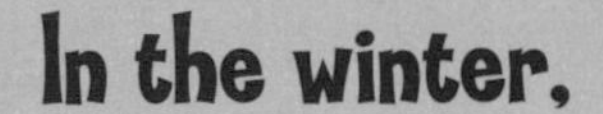

In the winter,
redwoods grow small cones. These cones contain lots of tiny seeds.

Redwood trees live a long time. A redwood might live to be 2,000 years old!

Redwoods live long because the bark is thick and strong. It does not get hurt easily by fire or fungus.

Baby redwoods often grow in circles around their parent tree.

Sadly, many redwoods have been cut down. People wanted their wood.

Another huge tree is
the giant sequoia.
Many giant sequoia grow in
the Sierra Nevada mountains
in California.

The giant sequoia
doesn't mind snow.

One hundred fifty years ago, giant sequoia seeds were brought to Europe. Today there are sequoias growing all over the world.

Native Americans called this tree *wawona* and *toos-pung-ish*.

Fires actually help the giant sequoia. Fires clear a space on the forest floor for baby trees to grow.

The giant sequoia are shorter and fatter than redwood trees.
They grow up to 300 feet high, and up to 30 feet in diameter.
Some live 3,000 years or more.

Giant sequoias are named after Sequoyah—a Native American who invented an alphabet in Cherokee.

The second largest tree in the world is named General Grant. It is a sequoia.

General Sherman is the name of the largest tree in the world. It is a giant sequoia that is still growing in California. People think it is about 2,300 years old!

Another famous sequoia is
Tunnel Log in Sequoia National Park.
This tree fell across a road.
It is so big that people
made a tunnel in it.
You can drive a car through it.

Sequoias need a lot of water.

No one is allowed to cut down a giant sequoia tree anymore.

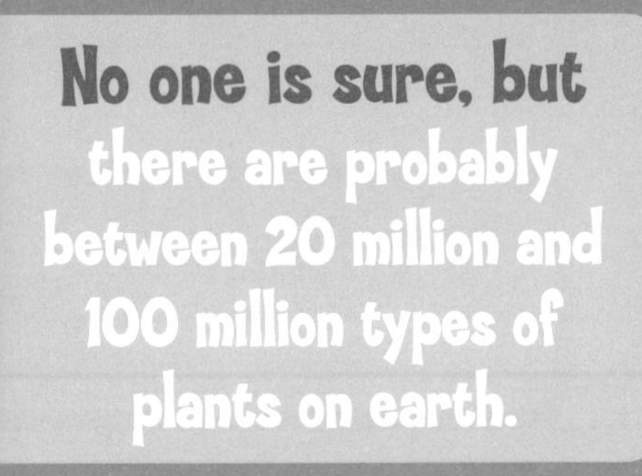

New types of plants are being discovered everyday, many of them in the world's rain forests.

God made plants all around us. God's plan is that we keep plants healthy and growing. Plants help us to stay healthy and grow too!

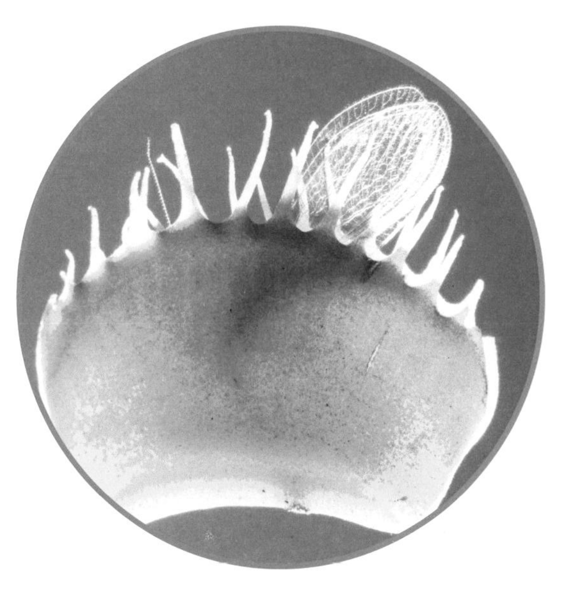

God had a wonderful plan when he made plants. He told Adam that man should respect and use creation, and he did.

People use plants for many things today too—people use plants as food, to make clothes, medicines, shelter, fuel, and tools to name a few.

Subject Index

love these other books about God's creation!